AFTER

AFTER

—— ✳ ——

Douglas Messerli

SUN & MOON PRESS
LOS ANGELES · 1998

Sun & Moon Press
A Program of The Contemporary Arts Educational Project, Inc.
a nonprofit corporation
6026 Wilshire Boulevard, Los Angeles, California 90036

This book was first published in paperback in 1998 by Sun & Moon Press
10 9 8 7 6 5 4 3 2 1
FIRST EDITION
©1998 by Douglas Messerli
Biographical material ©1998 by Sun & Moon Press
All rights reserved

This book was made possible, in part, through contributions to
The Contemporary Arts Educational Project, Inc.,
a nonprofit corporation

Some of these poems previously appeared in the magazines *Arshile, Avec, Cathay,
Chain, Conjunctions, Disturbed Guillotine, Hambone, Hot Bird, lower limit speech, Object,
Object Permanence* [England], *Proliferation, Ribot, Texture, The World,* and *Zyzzyva.*
Poems also appeared in the books *From the Other Side of the Century: A New American
Poetry 1960–1990* (Sun & Moon Press) and *The Gertrude Stein Awards in Innovative
American Poetry 1993–1994* (Sun & Moon Press), and in the Brazilian newspaper
Follha de San Paolo. "An Apple, A Day," was originally published as a chapbook,
An Apple, A Day, by Pyramid Atlantic (Riverdale, Maryland).

Cover: Sherrie Levine, *After Ludwig Kirchner,* 1982
Chromogenic-development (Ektacolor) print
Design: Katie Messborn
Typography: Guy Bennett

LIBRARY OF CONGRESS CATALOGING IN PUBLICATION DATA
Messerli, Douglas [1947]
After
p. cm—(Sun & Moon Classics: 131)
ISBN: 1-55713-347-6
I. Title. II. Series.
811'.54—dc20

Printed in the United States of America on acid-free paper.

CONTENTS

One cannot think in a language ignored by him.
—BARTOLMEO VANZETTI

In one lesson two cows were brought before the farmer: a Holstein from his own barn and, all the way from India, a Brahman. The interogater spoke: What do you see? I see a cow, said the farmer, pointing to the Brahman, and, he continued, gently outlining the black and white patterns upon the Holstein's back, a map of Mars!

In the second class two fish were tossed upon the fishwife's table, a flounder and a piranha from the mouth of the Amazon. She too was asked, What do you see? Without even blinking, she replied, I see dinner and some teeth.

Turning to his student, Elionisus sighed, Now, which of these workers' answers was closer to the truth?

—CLAUDE RICOCHET
from *The Analogies*

ORDER

And after

expression

is still

before to

what

comes next?

And next

is after

still before

to express

what comes?

And comes

to before

still after

what expresses

next?

And before

is next

to what

comes still

expressed after?

And is next

to come

after still

expresses what

before?

And expresses

after coming

a still what

before next?

MARINE

(after Mallarmé)

My face is a sponge and I
've sucked up everything I've seen.
To fly away! To slip off with the yelps of drunken gulls
and soar the soused skies!
Nothing, not the old bed
of flowers staring sourly at me
can keep my heart from getting doused
by the spray of sea, O knights!
Nor the deserting bulb of light
on the pasty-white page,
or the young boy swallowing
his mother's nipple with the milk.
I must flee! Suitcase sliding in the sway
of the heave, holding course for strange shores!
A boredom, without even hope,
that believes in the farewell flutter of hankies!
And, who knows, the sails, signaling to squalls,
may be those a wind cracks in the wrack,
missing, without a mainstay, mast, or bay in which to be
embraced. Still, O my heart, hear the sailor's chantey!

SITTING PRETTY

Were cuts

even as

before slices

touch. No distortion

perspires in the evidence.

Still feasts the keener

into a state of high

assumption. They deny

the separation of the brain

and state. That afternoons.

And even. A cadaver isn't written

into doze. But is in spite.

Already airs its occurrence

and tilts the empty

toward fuller, the incongruity

between the chairs and discomfort

of the rowdy uncles.

STRANGER

(after Baudelaire)

TELL me, young enigma, tell me, whom you love best, mother, father, sister, brother?

I have no father, no mother, no sister, no brother.

Your friends?

What are friends?

Your nation?

I don't even know what latitude it lies in.

Beauty?

I *could* love her, immortal goddess, yes.

Gold?

I hate gold as much as you hate god.

Stranger, what do you love then?

I love the clouds...the clouds passing overhead...up there...there...those astonishing puffs.

INDIFFERENCE

That is exactly not exact,

a point that points *out*

positing the apposite

as across, an apostate who believes

in his doubt, setting

upon a voyage of his own yawn.

The sun has become even

indifferent to sight

as white wicker put out

to fire it. There he settles

in a satisfying where

he, beached in that chair, knows I'm

witness, who cannot see—in the dark now

—that he has pitched his intense

glare back at the bent blind. Still

at the sill I fall

into his trip behind,

turn and become one

with another.

SALUTE

(After Mallarmé)

Nothing, this froth, pure poetry
Defining naught but vessel
To be so all at sea's sunk many
of school of sirens, their feet kicking air.

We're sailing, o my divers
Mates; I'm already at the poop
You at bow luxuriously
Lancing the waves of winter thunder

Reeling in the sweet intoxicating pitch
We've entered into fearlessly
I bear you, rising, a salute

Solitude, star, reef
To whatever importance you put
Upon the pale fret of our sail.

ENTRANCE

A move into

cuts one

away from

    the sudden gorge

ous man standing

at the edge

    of the emotion

    ally expressive face

    ing a door

turns back

to lean

upon a hunger

of the eyes

to which he agrees, knocking

any possibility away

that he will see

that deep impression.

WINDOWS

(after Baudelaire)

THROUGH an open window one never sees as much as through a closed. There is nothing more mysterious, poignant, pregnant, deceptive—more dazzling than a window lit by candlelight. What happens in a sunny street is always of less interest than what lies on the inside of the pane. In that black, back-lit square life survives, dreams, suffers.

Across the ocean of the roofs I see a middle-aged woman with furrowed face forever bending over something from which she will never part. Her story is spun from her clothes, aspect, acts, a myth that moves me as I tell it, to dissolve into tears.

If it had been an old man I might have made another tale up.

And it is good to go to bed having suffered in the skin of someone other than myself.

You may ask "Are you sure you've got the story right?" But does it really matter as long as it reveals what I feel, what I am.

WRISTS

They flicker to the trick

These pitched wrists

Palming plenty out to request

Love, largesse? Openness as in

Let's be, alone if necessary

With one or another mothering

That desire to smother

Dissimilarity and similitudinous

Which become us if they

Trust in the error between the two

The way they seam, angle-

Hooked as bill and coo. Get away

I want to say but stay put

To draw my soul afoot.

THE POET LAUREATE

(after Lorca after Spicer for Donald Allen once again)

An untouched figtree wants
to extend like a panther

stalking the shadow
of my poetry in echo

of its greenhorniness.
The moon argues with what dogs

her. She admits she's wrong
but still insists yesterday

was black as the morrow
might march round

my verdant crown. Where else
when I die will you look

for my heart? The figtree cries
in its advance, hideously extended.

BECKON

It is a pole

of snare, the matrix of

burning sometimes this hull

curved to wind, resembling

a circle aswim. Cranes

find their own contours

in the supple window

waving into the damp

shivering as might be

within parting

       bodies

       while thickets

       of quickened crickets

       crunched to wake

—so incomprehensibly—

into abstract concepts:

as fish is a word for

               passing fast shoals.

That is what means

the breeze uses to rise

out of its ash. Apparently

life spreads its seeds.

               Between an apple

and people ahead of where

it is about

      to fall

          there

is a sentence

seated on the windowsill.

We imagined the shake,

the unbearable being

of a still stiff drink

gone down to lap

it up. I'm trying to catch

the name of the completely

stripped beech

mathematically, as if the sign

were to hit the neck

that in seeking its kiss

sticks out

of that frame, escaping

itself like a downpour

of sweat. The glass

magnifies what

it encircles, the retina

of the ordinary ripped

from its socket

to sea across the shoals

the danger in sticking

        one's neck out

for the sake of it.

The meek shall inherit

the girth the fat let

      fall.   Come

back!

      Beckon sparks up

and stills the rub.

I CONFESS

(After Baudelaire)

THOSE late autumn afternoons. How poignant! Painfully so. For there are sensations that are sure to delight simply because they are so obscure. In the whole universe infinity has the sharpest edge.

What a pleasure to plunge the eyes then toward the sky and drown one's vision in the immensity of the sea. The silence, the solitude of this so chaste blue, the tiny sail hovering on the horizon, icon in its loneliness and isolation of my irreparable life, monotonous melody of these surges—all this and so much more reflects my thought, or this reflects me (since the ego is quickly lost in such reverie).... I say these things think, but I mean through music, through image without quibbles, syllogisms, conclusions.

But whether these spring from themselves or emanate from me, soon everything is too intense. Energy unabsorbed by pleasure can actually cause pain, a kind of unrest. Suddenly the nerves, excessively taut, transmit tortuously piercing vibrations through my brain and breast.

And now the profundity of sky, the undeviant blue, white light is irritating. The insensibility of sea, its placid liquid plash, is revolting! Ah, to reveal the beautiful one must suffer eternally—or flee. You pitiless old enchanter, enemy, Nature let me be! Stop your temptations and permit me at least my pride. To study beauty the artist must duel, howling at the horror before the blade strikes.

THE DESCENT

In is as nothing

alluded to presumably.

And there is known

with it now

somehow asking what

adds as substitution for

the round even

thought with persistence

summoning what knew

just as ice was served.

I didn't obviously!

What assumed lean was

attempting or had mentally

pointed down against.

What kind of staircase

did once went into? Anyway

by about, if I should wish,

we ignored as soon

aware approaching what

deserted stretched.

THE DOUBLE ROOM

(after Baudelaire)

SOME rooms are like dreams, spiritual rooms, where the dense air is tinted blue and pink.

There the soul can bathe in indulgence fragranted by desire and regret as at twilight, when all the blues become roseate, a sensate dream in eclipse. The furniture, elongated, languid, almost prostrate, seems to be dreaming itself, endowed with that sonambulistic existence we attribute to vegetables and precious rocks. Even the hangings speak the silent language of the heavens, of flowers, of suns about to set.

No abdomination of art upon the walls. Compared to the dream, to the obscure impression, art, with its statements, is blasphemy. In this room everything is bathed in a vagueness that produces harmony itself.

An infinitesimally small scent, exquisitely chosen, mingled with the slightest smell of damp, floats through this hothouse environment, cradling the spirit in sleep.

Over the window and bed muslin in diaphanous masses cascades into snowy cataracts. And on the bed lies the Idol, sovereign of my dreams. How has she come to be there? What magic power has placed her upon the throne of so much contemplation, so much pleasure? Does it matter? She is there, and I genuflect.

Yes, it is her eyes from which the flame pierces the darkening sky; those subtle and terrible spheres which I recognize by their awe-inspiring spite. They attract, subjugate, devour the gaze of the impudent. How often have I studied those black stars, arousing in me so much curiosity—and admiration.

To what benevolent demon do I owe all this mystery, silence, perfume, peace? O yes! What we usually call life, even at its fullest and happiest hours, cannot compare to what I now experience, minute by minute, instant by instant.

No! There are no more minutes, no seconds left! Time has disappeared. It is Eternity, an Eternity of pleasure that rules now.

But on the door a knock, a resounding clamor of the fist, and I, as in some infernal nightmare, feel a pitchfork being struck into my gut.

Enter the ghost, a sheriff come to torture me in the name of the law; or an infamous whore come with accusations to add to the petty pleasure of her life and the sorrow of mine; or a boy from the newsroom sent by the editor to bring back the sequel to my last installment.

That paradisiacal room along with the Idol, sovereign of my dreams (my Sylphid, as the great René used to say), all that enchantment has vanished with the brutal knock.

How awful! I remember. Yes, now I recall! This filthy hovel, the dwelling place of boredom is my own. Look at those stupid, dusty, dilapidated tables and chairs; no fire in the hearth, without even embers, soiled by spittle. And these excuses for windows with furrows traced by the rain across their muck; manuscripts half-erased; the almanac wherein my pencil has circled sinister dates.

And that intoxicating perfume wafting from a world beyond this? The stank of stale tobacco commingled with the sickening smell of must has taken its place. A rancid smell of waste.

In this narrow world, so full of disgust there is but one object of delight: a vial of opium, my terrible, old love, who like all mistresses, alas, betrays me as often as she takes me to her breast.

O yes, Time has returned to be reinstated as the sovereign lord of this place. And with him his entire retinue of Memories, Spasms, Fears, Agonies, Nightmares, Nerves, Rages, and Regrets, all have come back.

I can assure you that every second now is accented strongly by the clock, each after each calling out, "I am Life, unbearable, unmerciful Life!"

One second only in the lives of men announces good news, and that news puts terror into the heart of every man.

Yes, Time again rules; he has resumed his tyranny. He pokes me with his fork-shaped prod as if I were an ox: "Move on, you beast! Sweat slave, sweat! Live and be damned!"

THEN

Place of its volition

must be your eye

put to foot the off.

You walk the snap

desire needs for motive.

Some behind. And there

on the stick

is the survival after

all the fall has.

He is late to get

to yet is so far

away from the

future on the foot

of at. He is

so far back and you

into the wood

that wills its dark

bark as a dog of after

he will catch perhaps.

The summer forms

delay as end.

STAY, ELUSIVE SHADOW

(after Sor Juana Inés de la Cruz)

Stay, elusive shadow of myself,
handsome image whom I desire
beautiful illusion for whom I'd die
sweet fiction for whom I lie suffering.

If by your grace I'm magnetized
and my heart is drawn to your metal, why
with flattery, do you lead me on to feel
new love, since mockingly you flee my face?

You cannot boast that by your gifts
you as conquerer rule in tyranny;
for though you stretched the veins apart

which once your fantastic frame held
fast in my heart, it means nothing to my arms
if fancy makes a prison of the past.

EROS

In the gestures
the body pushes
the appearance
fatally
to the angel
burned
in glass.

Detached
from words
the sea
in the voice
arouses dimension
to escape
space.

Eyes step to
the chase
of the amorous
moths.

She speaks
an illusion
textually.

The tension
for a moment
moves the look
to an angle
parallel with.

The plump
ruin the drawn.

Flowing away
the pinched
compose the train
to take
up the vale.

The bent age.

From all round
anguish cries out
for further
taboo.

We create
the earth
that the human might
tastes
like the fowl.

To think
of an acorn
is to box
some in.

To think of in
is to acquire
a temple
of flesh.

The box
is only
an edge
upon which
to lay
hands.

BLESSINGS FROM THE MOON

(after Baudelaire)

THE Moon, whimsical as ever, shot a glance through the window where you lay sleeping in your crib, and said to herself, "This child I like."

Hushed, she descended her heavenly staircase, quietly passing through those panes. Stretching herself out over you with the litheness of a loving mother she lay her hues upon your face. The green pupils of your eyes have stood out against your pale white cheeks ever since. For upon receiving this night guest your eyes grew large permanently, and she, in response, so gently grasped your neck that you shall never be troubled with tears again.

In the swelling of her breast, the Moon filled your whole room, however, with a phosphorescence that fell upon its surfaces in a residue of poisonous gold dust. And so illuminated, the room itself seemed to speak. "You shall suffer the consequences of this kiss. Although you be a beauty, it shall be in my style, for you shall love only what I love and what loves me: the clouds over the sea on the still, still night; the ocean's immensity; streams formless and intricately complex; places where you cannot be where lovers, whom you shall never meet, come to love; monstrously misshapen flowers; perfumes that drive men into delirium; convulsing cats that collapse and curl up on grand pianos groaning like sopranos who in singing shriek!

And you shall be loved by my lovers, in turn, courted by my courtiers. Those with green eyes shall crown you their queen, those who I have also touched in their sleep, who love oceans, blue-green seas, erratically-ribboned rivers, places where they can never be with women who they shall never meet, night flowers blooming like the censers of some exotic ritual or religion, fragrances that force men to forsake their beliefs, savage and sensuous beasts which serve as signs of their own insanity.

That, my poor, cursed child, is why I lie at your feet, seeking to soak up some scrap of knowledge through you, predestined daughter, of the Divinity, that horrible hag of a night nurse who locks all lunatics away from me.

PALL

It is be

that confects the cover

exegesis struts:

a lash that springs

out of worry into

partitioning, a keel

of plea. Old hulk

hire a shadow!

Take these avenues

into your knees!

Going down, release

the ribbon of the craft.

Out will come the whole seen

as coming out, a hiss of slender

spines that hit the street.

All cuts in, slows, evades,

flinches. I put off feet

for the fact of after.

In the distance a trained

whistle for the construct.

I thought you were following

but where, in toting up the dots,

has the hedge gone off? I'm suspicious

yes suspicious about the dangle

that raises such high spite.

Gone is the pause of past.

Nothing but the strand

of watery-blue

eyes leaning on a paratactic

hirsute in the moonlight

can let me know exactly

what you keen

so eagerly as for what

the seminal smile

before the notch.

This heart is due

to pedal black

but like a moth

batters hit to light.

FOR ROBERT DELAUNAY

(after Arp)

around your bed two suns soar
day's sun and night's

you're feeling better looking well
a bulldozer eating vitamins

open the windows and take a look
nights tower and days

bed's no place for a jet
come light the fire and the winking star

EDGE

Things eclipse and summit hewn

to would parts

where just the matter

's grown to stump. Near sticks

to the tongue as warnings

of what gaped?

NOSTALGIA

(after Ungaretti)

When
the night
a little before spring
passes
and no one else does

Paris acquires
an obscure color
of pity

On a bridge
I note
the endless
silence
of a thin
child

Our deaths
are fond
of each other

And we stay
as if carried off

LOVE SONG

Arouse closes where

Triumph knuckles.

Clasp devotes

Stamp and buttress.

Groins wheeze flap.

Nouns point at where

Risk insists

On riven.

The truth of penetration

Is of course—

A blundering

Of adequation. Possession

Passes as a rapid

Finger dance. It is

The extent of the infallible,

The fall of it. Be frantic

In the pencil

Ing. I can

Put in what is like

The word toward

Mouth subvocalized

To pharynx, tongue and

Hips of modulation.

No one stays

In English twice. Every kind

Of swearing is uncertainty

Slurred as words, sober chords

Of cut. Pleasantries

Exchanged as wrist, kissed.

The forehead reported sample,

And phrased affable as frank.

A SHADY AFTERNOON

(After Ovid)

A day of humidity, an afternoon of shade
limbs falling where the couch sinks to embrace.
The blinds are drawn fast—but one
slapping in the sun allows a lie of light
in, light as a virgin stand of trees
fluttering, fades as Phoebus says farewell
day to even turning;
a light that cloaks the shy sisters
if they are still undressed, desiring to be alone yet—
  Look!
Here comes Corinna
in her night shirt, lifting with the body's movements
hair floating to the base of her neck
in the heroic style in which Semiramis dressed
to cross the border of her wedding bed.
And so dressed Lais, the princess
who pleased so many men.

I ripped her shift, it was so thin
barely bruising the beauty beneath
while she struggled so to gather it again—
to win the silly scuffle
then gave in—a self-betrayal.
Her slip had fallen.
And suddenly she stood simply before me.
How could I fail to flatter, praising her arms, her
  shoulders

and her waiting breasts, waiting
now kissed erect...and below
the long, lovely thighs of a girl
about to become—why
say more? Everything was perfect. I took her
straight. What next? Who doesn't remember?
Exhausted, we slept.
Were every afternoon so shady.

THIS LAID OUT

This laid out
on the breathing skin
hesitatingly spoken
as rustle
recasts the sheet
in aftermath
like layers
of lost perspiration
with the animated gesture
to loose the self,

the pants
on the chair
bending with the avalanche
of flesh to sock the foot
as bruise brings a bout
to mug the coffee with.

ONCE MORE I HAVE SEEN
THE ASTONISHING CHILD...

(after Paul Verlaine)

Once more I have seen the astonishing child; it seemed
That it relieved my heart of its last pain
Assuring me that through exquisite suffering
Of the desired death one day I'll be at rest.

The perfectly pointed arch with its repeating thrust
Through these fervent moments has aroused me
Against the languid little fantasies of boring hesitance,
And all my Christian blood now sings the pure hymn.

I see, I hear again. The law of rite. How sweet!
To have the gift to cock the ears and behold once more,
I will hear and see perpetually! The voice of all good *penseés*

Summoning the innocent future. Silent and wise.
How I will love as I press this second to me,
Those lovely little hands that close our eyes.

HERO AND ANTAGONIST

Traveling

where I bored

the proscenium

with my hands

the hero

committed

inexplicably the play

little by little

and sometimes

I broke the pitcher

and rose

under the pretext

of trying to slash—

but these were lands

impossible to pick.

I was separated,

a character

who had made

hate the rumor.

Suddenly the cone

of the endless corridor

I wandered.

All at once

the freedom, the freedom

of aluminum chairs

over which

my silhouette

was thrown

in fury,

venetian windows

where beats

wet street lamps

and the bleeding

crack under the weight

of all those columns.

They cry.

There are branches still

full of birds

that lay

black eyes.

Young girls shake

the sharp plants

enough to foam

the bottle.

He's the one snarling.

He's visible.

The women lean

from the ledges.

THE VOLCANO

(after Mallarmé)

By your cloud still struck
Low with lava and ash
Into the enslaving echo
Of the worthless blast

What a hollow wreck (still spuming,
but with a drool) as you know
Towering over the destruction
Consumated in its riven mast.

Or was it in a rage
Of some great perdition
That this abyss was so vainly whipped up

With white hair falling
Down so stingily to drown
the cheeks of a child siren.

ARROWS

(for St. Valentine)

The leap

of knowing to

its body

hedges

to right stand

so pelt we jumped

beyond the string

to laughter. Sunk

in steel time

this is crumble

to cement dreadnaught.

The charcoal is his rent

as threadage ochres on

its thicket, eyes

out there blackening

with blink and quick

'ens it to pottage

of its dotter.

What buck lasts

to pit the chart

of cat against

chatter? Cold as out.

The fire has. And sit

at arm in

the adage:

pods collect

in specks

to grease

the spoken head

that bulbs the bend

to hand. It is astor.

A bed of magnesium

the rock the guy has

put to whit you fly

across, the flood

of this wicket. The

dropout mothers brass.

Crystals sweat

into debt or

cancels what rib

sticks to

against the stiff

snuff of breath—

unless

is too a blade

dogbrick loped

to bank of

lessens. That afterward

opens glass of

was it airlock,

war, or a glisten

in the eye

of acceptance?

Lean is

leaning on the leaner

reef to fix

in paper impress

what bog annoyed

as horn to

warning

against close.

Struggles' cheap

to may be brush.

A map dozes.

Lava is a crisis

of the stars, a piece

cast lower than

the type of region

a degree durates.

The gloss of eucalyptus

sheens as surface

where light falls

off of shaken

beyond the hedge

what truth fences

in the get.

Climbing it's

slow-made of

liars, snail-like

into glassy slag

as hem puckers

pup to lap slapped

down to simple

snipe at heal

of whose or

deal of Yes.

The Elect

malts trim

to sew meet

umbrage with penned

simmers of barrettes

the hair is heir to.

Your soapstone high

and elk hew yawn

of feather hangs

on here as fast

said actual

as you did not.

The even be

is so freedom,

singing in the dark

part of mutter's

mobile.

Flip opens sneeze

as activities of honks.

The geese

pass the moon

by an I of to

the distance crossed.

Trammel seizes oar

and guides the scotch

by nature to crab life.

Hear on the breaches….

the sirens

coped out

and spoke about

their capture

as if story

was the fish,

leaving sound

to bore into

meaning.

Still you were.

The very wheat

of nod

and grain

of sod

in rain

of sodom

's tears,

the germ

of nation's

reason

for all seasons.

I'VE BOUGHT YOU, I ADMIT IT

(after Michelangelo)

I've bought you, I admit it, at great cost
a little something, which smells sweetly,
because I often get to know a street by its scent.
Wherever you may be, wherever I am,
I'm certain beyond a doubt.
If you hide from me, I'll forgive you.
Carrying this with you, on your way,
I'll find you, even if I'm blind as a bat.

SHADOWS

Shadows with before

let breathe reflect

condemned as full

gathers light upon

the profoundest tip

surfacing impediments

of flattened midnight

in its expect.

Now I watch the taste

of recognition frontal

as the note drawn out

of pocket strikes

the flanks and wedges

glimmer promising

the pout of day's lip.

I raise my shuteye

to the angle vagrant

as instruct swills

the wary grip, full

of reason to rip

the pamper off of it.

You and your company

part lines without

subtraction, retaining

the coherence as it rages,

clue to the twist

Due suffered in the lapse.

This has happened once

before conformity exploded

want as a train pulling

Out to circle back

to identical waves

of madness, the dream

Of suggestion's prospect.

Each is a disaster.

The sun sets on the moon.

DOG AND BOTTLE

(after Baudelaire)

HERE my good doggie, my dear doggie, my sweet little one, smell this superb scent from the most select of the city's *perfumeries*.

And the dog, with wagging tail, the way these creatures, I believe, signify their smiles and laughs, came to me to put his snub snout to the bottle I'd unplugged; then, backed way in fright, with reproachful barks.

Ah! you miserable mut, if I had put a packet of excrement before your nose you might have inhaled and ingested it even in delight. So it is with the public to whom one should never proffer a delicate fragrance that will infuriate some when, it seems, the smell from the sewers pleases everyone.

NARRATIVITY

Slide into afternoon was anything but

down and out

seedy music automatically

was the muse itself. She (the program)

is he really—and since you asked

it's true the spin I am already in

is the death of dance. So I stand

still

understand which gets no where?

In a trance like ennui

gone to town. You jerk.

I jerk. We all

crawl away from the table

to pretty and properly frilly and cute

couches, chairs, and laps

all out of breath

and believe you me.

There is an elm tree

which was spared

the Dutch disease

in the yard

in front

of the little plot

which will bury me.

So forget narrativity!

There was never a tree

as lovely as that

I just made up

And we went home together

this delicious decidious and me

and lived for eternity

in a hut

I cut

it into.

But meanwhile it was.

Rain. A demand of homage.

Someone got drunk

by mistake

and lay for days

in the belly of his host.

Another.

And a couple in the corner

over and over

"What would a holiday be without Billie?"

We would know that.

We would sing along.

We would dance.

We would.

In the little hut.

And meanwhile.

Snow. Someone demanded a cover.

(He was getting cold

or older and older

before our eyes

could recognize

each other.)

Isn't it time to go someone asked?

Since everyone already had.

QUIET

(after Ungaretti)

The grape is ripe, the field furrowed,

From the clouds the mountain has loosed itself.

Over summer's dusty mirrors
The shadows collapse.

Between uncertain fingers
Light clears
Lengthens

The painful fight of swallows
Is the last tear.

THE TRIP

Look this figure

this mirror

this photo

(I tripped)

this shoulder

offered

this slowness

this spiral

(his mark)

I can see

turning

(his turning)

this owl

(I tripped)

these moths

so tired

the pages

we walked

this liquid

unlistening

voice

this second

I recall

this yes at

that age

this telling

of hands

they'd trip.

SCARED

(after Vallejo)

This spurt frightens me,
memorable, masterful, implacable
cruel sweetness. It scares me.
This house is perfectly pleasing, the whole
reason for this condition of not knowing where to go.

Let's not enter. I fear the present, the allowance
to return at any moment, across blasted bridges.
I won't push any further, sweet sir,
gallant reflection, sad
song of skeleton bones.

How peacefully, he of this enchanted house
spends my quicksilver, and plugs
my orifices leading
to a dried-out actuality.

The spurt that has no taste of the future,
frightens me, makes me tremble.
Gallant reflection, I won't go any further.
Blond sad sack of bones, boo! boo!

IT means

splinter, thick caned

to matt, a crate to carrion.

It means the bridge of hunk,

a ratchet to hurl that animal

fat at, a buckle of the lift

ing belly that shadows the

cave in to reversal: flood

of sulky blood on wash

as chucker sizes pet

their sunsets, a whale

of a lip scud to soak

in oaken cask, borne

out in the escarpments

that batten lap. Come

my whisker, wicked as

a blister of the wax!

INSERT

(after Mallarmé)

Insert me into your tale
It's an embarrassed hero
Who hasn't yet set bare feet
To some turf of your territory.

Against your high and mighty glaciers
I know of no sinner so innocent
To not have been scared off
By your haughty whoop of having won.

Tell me if I'm not gay enough
Thunder and jewels at my hub
To see the air cut by your stares

Cross your so easily dispersed domains
As scarlet dies to rake the wheels
At twilight of my lonely carriage there.

RAISING THE ROOF

Sound that by

means abut

rights coincidence

and flies to take

the air. A brick sides

to corner. The window

ever down spaces in

the pinning

channel of what said.

The room is won by who

to nailing lodges

wait as if holding

brittle in the tug.

Dimly's seen as fending

off the laugh. They move

to center traps that fail

the fingerings—and brings

down the house

as curtains up.

THE TALE OF THE LITTLE RED HAT

(after Vladimir Mayakovsky)

Once upon a time there was a Cadet[*]
a little Cadet who had a red hat.

But apart from that hat that capped
his head there was in him no shred of red.

But quick as revolution began
The Cadet ran home to get his red

tam. They all lived happily—
Brother, Father and Cadet granddad—

as they had until one day a wind blew
right through his hair to tear the red

hat from his head and reveal his Black
roots. The revolting red wolf got his licks

of the boots and ate his way up to that Cadet's
knees but was still so starved he carved

up the heart. So please when you're about to start
politics don't forget how that Cadet got et.

[*] Cadet was the nickname for the Constitutional Democrats, the
party of the political Center.

THOSE WHO PAID

The tongues

of those who've

tried to talk

too often have

been taken out

and tied

to belt.

The construction crews

stop Smetana-ing

and flow

with the river

into which

they're tossed.

Chorus boys go home

again with fevers

for trombones, sliding

into bed and blasting

through the rooftops

to rain

down as pennies

upon the poor

sweepers-up.

They're electrified

by the eels

left in the foot

steps of those

who had to pay.

THE CROCUS

(after Apollinaire)

The meadow is pretty in autumn but full
Of poison the calm cows
gradually graze on
Crocus ringed in lilac
Like your eyes efflorescing
In their violet shadowed rings like autumn
Through your eyes my life little by little sucks death in

School kids in a fracas arrive
Playing harmonicas in denim dickeys
To pluck and cradle the crocus like mothers
Daughters of their daughters they share the color
of your eyes fluttering like flowers in the demented skies

Softly the cowboy sings
While the slow lowing beasts leave
The land fall forever flowered so evilly

A DRIFT

A drift into

set

keeps the stay

fast to let

what sent

leaves

again, as black

on back to

point at   .

         the distances

between

folding in

and hold.

We are told

that spring

follows

in the tight

curl of

the dried

up, out of it

coming to

no conclusions

but the

enticing

ice

of

turning

in.

SNOW WHITE

(after Apollinaire)

Angels angels in the sky
One is dressed as officer
One is dressed as chef
And the others sing

Bright officer, color of the sky
Long after Christmas spring will softly bring
A shining sun to regale you
  A shining sun

The chef plucks the geese

Ah! the vault of snow
The fall and no
Sweetheart to enter my embrace

EVEN

The there

is caved.

The rock

moved to stillness. Burn

hovers to a dwindle.

I have a cloud smoking

on the horizon

-tal. Time lies

to the sun.

Bark lets listen.

SCROOGE

(after Jules Laforgue)

Noel! Noel? I hear bells in the night
And to these unbelieving leaves put my pen.
O sing memories! All arrogance takes flight
And by bitterness I'm overwhelmed again.

Ah! the night voices chanting Noel!
Tranform me from knave—which, out there, is lit—
With reproach so tender, sweet, maternal
That my heart, too full, heaves behind my tits…

And for a long while in the darkening
I am the pariah of the human race
Whom the wind in this squalid hole harkens
To join the celebration of some far off place.

GOING PLACES

Excursion becomes

what form

of linkage? *We* expect

a place of skin

that seems horizon.

Trouble is recorded

in address. *You* are

the hope of being

and *I* the ravenous

raven of recall.

The past is not

at home when

the present is received.

THE JOKER

(after Baudelaire)

THE bedlam of New Year's: now churned up to a chaos by carriages, thousands of them—festooned in shining ornaments and sweets—smothered in a desparate lust; the frenzied officiousness of cities set on prying into the most private of states.

In the center of all this hubub a donkey trots to whip of a tramp. At the corner the donkey is met by a totally tailored gent, groomed, gloved, torturously necktied—in clothes that wear him, who with all due ceremony bows to the beast: "May the New Year bring you happiness and wealth!" And with that he turns fatuously back to his friends in expectation, evidently, of applause.

The donkey paid no attention at all to this perfectly dressed practical joker and went on his way where the whip took him.

But I was seized by a fit of angry disgust. For it seemed to me suddenly that into that monkey-dressed man was compressed all the wit of France.

FENCE

Peculiar like a space
of flipped alternative
forgetting thus had faded.
The scene was one I camera-eyed

with sounds repeatedly wished
somewhere before a long
way back, its inconsequence
walking beside the foot

which previously had commenced.
In all the surface there was
wondering a flash of last minute
paradigm reckoned as the blurr

of the distract, particularizing
fence as echoes of the yet
where in the absence
is what was never lost.

SPLEEN

(after Baudelaire)

When the sky lays as heavy as a thick woolen blanket
Upon a sick soul bored out of his head
And, seeming to embrace everything in sight,
Suffocates in a darkness blacker than night,

When the earth turns into a dank
Prison where Hope flaps its frail wings
Upon the walls and beats on
The rotting ceiling with her head,

When rain spreads trails so immense
That they imitate prison bars
And in the back of the mind a horde
Of spiders spin their webs—

Bells leap furiously out
To catapult their awful racket up to heaven
Like the incessant wail of ghosts
Without a house

And long hearses unaccompanied by drum
File slowly through my heart; fallen Hope
Cries out and that selfish despot Pain
Plants a black flag in my brain.

AN APPLE, A DAY

_____

THE whisper of night's overhead
doves curving wings increase
by as many
as branches the poplar.
The tree flies off
its roots, topples
to put this missle
in its bark: love
is over
powering.

_____

THE morning's ours
the night
it stabs
with light
rays up
everyone!

_____

THERE is a space
between the pace
of the eating
away of place

where the body is about
to sail into and its
stasis. Standing it still
moves.

———————————

AN apple, a day
an other
and you can't quite
bite into anymore
these days
are short
as stem
to core. Didn't it use
to mean you knew
it was delicious
to be between?

———————————

THE slow
now's won
by young wait
-ing to become
old quicker
than they know
it isn't
a head
but behind
that gets thicker.

———————

WE are ours
-elves working round
the clock to define
the shape of time
larger than lives
within the smallest acts
of a head.

———————

ONCE upon time
you are drawn in
to present
that past
its own future
unto those who will
have been you.

———————

WE all know a yes
that says it
with e
-nough belief
he who can
not bottle up
any more needs
to pour in relief
what's inside out

the mouth
in a shout
of doubt.

———————

NEIN lives
in a yes
-terday that again
attentuates! Now I go
on ego as I did id.

CONTEMPLATION

(after Baudelaire)

Be wise, sweet Sorrow, be more still.
You desired the end of day; it's coming, here
The obscure air's enveloping the atmosphere
Portending peace to some, others worry

While the vile multitudes obey now
The lash of torture's pleasure, never
Released, pick up remorse once more in servile celebration.
Sorrow, take my hand, let's go this way

Far from sight. Lean the dear departed years
in their outdated dresses against the scaffolds
of the sky. Peering through deep waters Regret

Smiles. Under an arch the sun sleeps, moribund.
And from the East, long shroud trailing after—
Listen deary—Night softly shuffles in.

DESCENT

(after Milton)

Descend if rightly

Following above

The meaning

Of old before

Return

Lest from

Dismounted

Erroneousness

Half yet within

Standing more

To hoarse

In evil

Darkness

Visited by purples

Of that wild

As reap the harp

And her soul.

Say the affable

Apostasy to those

In Paradise

Charged so easily

As if the story

Heard in admiration

With so much

Confusion sprung

A blessedness.

The doubts

Led on

What nearer

Went before yet

Score proceeded

To what

Things above our

Knowing embrace.

DOING TIME

(after Vallejo)

Time Time.

Noon asphyxiated in night air.
A boring joke of the barracks choking
time time time time time.

Was Was.

Cocks song scratched out futilely.
Mouth of clear day conjugates
was was was was.

Morrow Morrow.

The still warm rest of being.
The present thinks it can hold me for
morrow morrow morrow morrow.

Name Name

What's it called that pricks us with goose bumps?
It's called Thesame that suffers
name name name and namE.

THE ACT

for Howard

I action the calling

standing to another

myth performance makes,

*b*eering to give the empty its sides.

You promise the around,

leaving latitude to our now

vast there, the titular kindle

where the genial jostles

the sterilized guise.

       Slipping

warbles cliffs,

radiating a sway

that banters

berserkly aside the seize,

chalking the squeal

up to inclination.

Are you headed?

The lines of trajectory

fall upon the street

light and lit up

as a spill.

I call the

action to another

stand performance mythologizes.

THE EXTREMES

*(after Rae Armantrout, as translated from
American into French and out of it again)*

Traveling into the desert
  the term is used up

  "zero's scenery"

  slivers of earth's rim
attract the eyes once more

to approach these blades!

  lines that cross whatever
beings vanish into / enflame

the enchanted edges of presence

HIT

Pit of down for someone takes

The makeup as in cover, cowered

By the box of circumstantial

Hate late night redresses

For the day, the way you were

Not what was

In light but weakly

Worn out as a coat

That keeps whether

Or not way from

Thin skin. It beads

A little to tip

Tongue on lip when stealing

Its voice for the healing.

LED THROUGH MANY YEARS

(after Michelangelo)

Led through many years to my last hours
Too late, o world, I know of your delights:
The peace you don't have, you promise others,
And that repose is dead before its birth.
The shame and dread
Of age, prescribed
By stars, only revives me
To the old and sweet mistakes,
The result of too long a life
which slays the soul, and leaves the old man laughing.
The dice of heaven, the proof's
in me, can bring only better luck
for he who presses the hand of death.

SILENCE

Drift—an intuition

has been mended

to affix, beyond attract

was alight

as if meaning were a hitch

to the variant approaching

of the sudden screech

a loud ripping of what is now

permitted: nothing

we could say

could keep silence off....

SHAME

(after Rimbaud)

As long as the blade
Hasn't sliced through brain
This tubby leak-colored clump
Of old rotten odors—

(Ah! But they really should
Cut off his lips—ears—nose
Whole belly! And save!—
O that's good—both stalks of leg)

Yes! I truly believe
Until the blade overhead
The stones at his flank
The fire in the gut

Are released
This bratty little beast
Will not for one second
Cease his mischief

And like a civet cat
Will piss along his path.
Oh God! grant when the time
Comes at least a prayer will rise up!

TAKE FRIGHT

Dawn is what begins

to know the weapon

's in a head

like structure

collapsing to recover

reason into language,

dreading the tiny place

that accepts gaze.

Breathing is slow.

The ashes already

full of his shadow

oh how to compensate!

The explosion is so far

away. Was. Awakened

actually that memory.

Night keeps finding us.

FOR LOVE'S BOOK

(after Jules Laforgue)

I may die tomorrow and still I haven't loved.
My lips have never touched a woman's.
None has proposed with eyes to give her spirit.
None in the act of love has taken me to heart.

I have suffered though for all nature
For beings, wind, flowers, sky,
Suffered through every minute ending of my nerves,
Suffered to purify my still impure soul.

I've spat at love, flayed the flesh.
Mad with pride, I've stood stiff against all living.
And alone upon this earth defied
The slavery of my instincts with bitter laughs

Everywhere, at salons, the theatre, the church
Before those frigid folks, the grand gentlemen of pol-
    ished fingers
And women with gentle, jealous, haughty eyes
And tender sensibilities so exquisite and ready to be
    raped.

I've thought: all of these have come to it. I've heard
in their rituals the roars of filthy, fucking beasts.
So much shit to waddle through for such a few minutes!
Men, behave yourselves! Women, flutter away!

THE BLACK FISH

The galls call

a wind like the pass

of two boys who laugh

at the gangle. Then

sprawls, calling

to their hunger:

the black fish

beneath their feet.

THE ACQUAINTANCE

(after Robert Frost)

I have been, I have
walked, I have outwalked.
I have looked, I have passed
And dropped my eyes.
I have stood still
When far away,
Come to houses
But not to call
And further still
One luminous clock
Proclaimed the time
Taken to be.

SEIZURE

Then that is

what makes us

reach still more

and I

the chocked

obscure, wrestling

to bring finally

a wound

as the sentence

the silence

falls upon

watch it gather

in the deep

pillows, the dreams

of a tongue

that extend

to roof

like a hand

birds prefer

to fly from—

what light!

announces

syllables that circulate

the secret babble

carried inside

someone else's sin

you've stolen from.

BAD THOUGHTS

(after Jules Supervielle)

Don't be shocked,
Close your eyes
Until they turn
Truly to stone.

Leave your heart alone
Although it stops.
It beats solely for itself
from a secret inclination of its own.

Your hands will spread out
from the frozen block
and your brow will be bare
as a great square between
two occupied armies.

FEVER

The long fever

refuses to tow

appearance. It paints

by siding with the victim.

The flush "keeps the guard

up" to conceal excursion.

It pastes sound upon the temple

without entering intuit. Glisten

does as does shining in a glimmer.

O what an echo! On the surface

is a paleolithic ripple, guppy

of the cataclysmic crack

in that gap between

not being here and enter

into the room to open

windows. O that bright

light as feather

ticks to chin and bares it,

pointing out the roseate

reality that branches a complexion.

The quiet still shakes

in the dizzy mourning

that melts the marrow

it felt so cold.

NARCISSUS

(After Spicer after Lorca)

Poor Narcissus

dim heart meeting

river, at the edge

I'll lay above the

ripples of your nipples

staring into your white

eyes where butterflies

flatten the mirror

against your face. The frogs

croak out of surface

that pours sorrow

into what is left

of you.

CLOSURE

Enmeshment is an enter

ing that twines the two as through

a closed screen he who on the

other side can cut but I

in place bend to press against

my breast informing net and

guest the door is shut.

DESPAIR

(after Baudelaire)

THE withered old woman beamed with happiness when she saw the pretty child whom everyone wished to amuse and everyone wanted to please. Such a lovely creature, so fragile, just like the little old woman, and, yes, similarly without hair and teeth.

She went up to the infant, ready to smile, to contort her face amusingly.

Terrified, the child struggled to be free of the kind, old woman's caresses, filling the house with his shrieks.

The decrepit woman crept back into the corner crying: "The age of pleasing is past for tired old ladies. Once I delighted the innocent at least, but now even a babe whom I would love can't stand my sight."

A SLEEP

The deer have tracked

the angle

it guards

to soft earth.

The stars rain

all night, all night

we hardly saw

anything in sight

this page, these words.

Douglas Messerli

Born in 1947, Douglas Messerli has published several books of poetry, including *Dinner on the Lawn, Some Distance, River to Rivet: A Manifesto, Maxims from My Mother's Milk/Hymns to Him,* and two volumes of his projected trilogy, *The Structure of Destruction* (*Along Without* and *The Walls Come True: An Opera for Spoken Voices*). Under the name Kier Peters, he has written some ten plays, including *The Confirmation, A Dog Tries to Kiss the Sky, Family,* and *Intentional Coincidence.* Michael Kowalski's opera *Still in Love,* based on Peters' *Past Present Future Tense,* was recently released on CD.

As founder and publisher of Sun & Moon Press, Messerli has edited over 300 titles, including *From the Other Side of the Century: A New American Poetry 1960–1990, 50 × 2: A Celebration of Sun & Moon Classics,* and numerous works of Djuna Barnes. For New Directions he edited *"Language" Poetries*; and for Sun & Moon he edits the annual *Gertrude Stein Awards in Innovative American Poetry.* In 1994 he was awarded the Harry Ford Editing Award, given in recognition of an ongoing commitment to the publication and promotion of contemporary American poetry.

SELECTED SUN & MOON CLASSICS

BARRETT WATTEN [USA]
  Frame (1971–1991) 117 (1-55713-239-9, $13.95)

MAC WELLMAN [USA]
  The Land Beyond the Forest: Dracula AND *Swoop* 112
  (1-55713-228-3, $12.95)
  Two Plays: A Murder of Crows AND *The Hyacinth Macaw* 62
  (1-55713-197-X, $11.95)

JOHN WIENERS [USA]
  707 Scott Street 106 (1-55713-252-6, $12.95)

ÉMILE ZOLA [France]
  The Belly of Paris 70 (1-55713-066-3, $14.95)

*

Individuals order from:
Sun & Moon Press
6026 Wilshire Boulevard
Los Angeles, California 90036
213-857-1115

Libraries and Bookstores in the United States and Canada
should order from:
Consortium Book Sales & Distribution
1045 Westgate Drive, Suite 90
Saint Paul, Minnesota 55114-1065
800-283-3572
FAX 612-221-0124

Libraries and Bookstores in the United Kingdom and on the Continent
should order from:
Password Books Ltd.
23 New Mount Street
Manchester M4 4DE, ENGLAND
0161 953 4009
INTERNATIONAL +44 61 953-4009
0161 953 4090